Shoes

The Sound of SH

By Peg Ballard

The **Child's World**®

Shelly needed new shoes.

Mom took Shelly shopping.

Shelly saw many shoes.

She saw pink shoes.

She saw blue shoes.

She saw black shoes.

She saw brown shoes.

She saw shiny shoes.

Shelly picked blue shoes.

Shelly showed Dad her new shoes.

Word List

she	shoes
Shelly	shopping
shiny	showed

Note to Parents and Educators

Welcome to Wonder Books® Phonics Readers! These books are based on current research that supports the idea that our brains detect patterns rather than apply rules. This means that children learn to read more easily when they are taught the familiar spelling patterns found in English. As children progress in their reading, they can use these spelling patterns to figure out more complex words.

The Phonics Readers texts provide the opportunity to practice and apply knowledge of the sounds in natural language. The ten books on the long and short vowels introduce the sounds using familiar onsets and *rimes*, or spelling patterns, for reinforcement. The letter(s) before the vowel in a word are considered the onset. Changing the onset allows the consonant books in the series to maintain the practice and reinforcement of the rimes. The repeated use of a word or phrase reinforces the target sound.

As an example, the word "cat" might be used to present the short "a" sound, with the letter "c" being the onset and "–at" being the rime. This approach provides practice and reinforcement for the short "a" sound, since there are many familiar words with the "–at" rime.

The number on the spine of each book facilitates arranging the books in the order in which the sounds are learned. The books can also be arranged into groups of long vowels, short vowels, consonants, and blends. All the books in each grouping have their numbers printed in the same color on the spine. The books can be grouped and regrouped easily and quickly, depending on the teacher's needs.

The stories and accompanying photographs in this series are based on time-honored concepts in children's literature: Well-written, engaging texts and colorful, high-quality photographs combine to produce books that children want to read again and again.

Dr. Peg Ballard
Minnesota State University, Mankato, MN

About the Authors

Dr. Peg Ballard holds a PhD from Purdue University and is an associate professor in the department of curriculum & instruction at Minnesota State University. Her area of expertise is diagnosis and remediation of reading difficulties. Dr. Ballard serves as a curriculum consultant and facilitator for school districts adopting new literacy programs. She has conducted in-service workshops and conference presentations on phonics instruction, literacy assessment and evaluation, and comprehension strategies.

Photo Credits

All photos © copyright: Romie Flanagan/Flanagan Publishing Services.

Special thanks to the Gaddis-Gayden family

Photo Research: Alice Flanagan
Design and production: Herman Adler Design Group

Library of Congress Cataloging-in-Publication Data

Ballard, Peg.
    Shoes : the sound of "sh" / by Peg Ballard.
    p. cm. — (Wonder books)
    Summary : Simple text and repetition of the letters "sh" help readers
learn how to use this sound.
    ISBN 1-56766-726-0 (lib. bdg. : alk. paper)
    [1. Shoes Fiction. 2. Alphabet.] I. Title. II. Series: Wonder books
(Chanhassen, Minn.)
PZ7.B21195Sh   1999
[E]—dc21
                                                99-31460
                                                CIP

OCT '06 SOUTH HILL